KU-120-528

This book belongs to

....

....

Written by Rachel Elliot
Illustrated by Julia Seal
Edited by Catherine Ard
Designed by Nicola Moore
Production by Richard Wheeler
Gymnastics consultant: Carol Malone

First published by Parragon in 2012
Parragon
Queen Street House
4 Queen Street
Bath BA1 1HE, UK

Copyright © Parragon Books Ltd 2012

All rights reserved. No part of this publication may be reproduced,
stored in a retrieval system, or transmitted, in any form or by any means,
electronic, mechanical, photocopying, recording, or otherwise, without
the prior permission of the copyright holder.

ISBN 978-1-4454-5638-6

Printed in China

The Littlest Gymnast

Emily and her friends love gym club.

They go every day after school.

Emily is the
smallest gymnast
in the club.

Everyone in gym club can do something special.

Everyone except Emily.

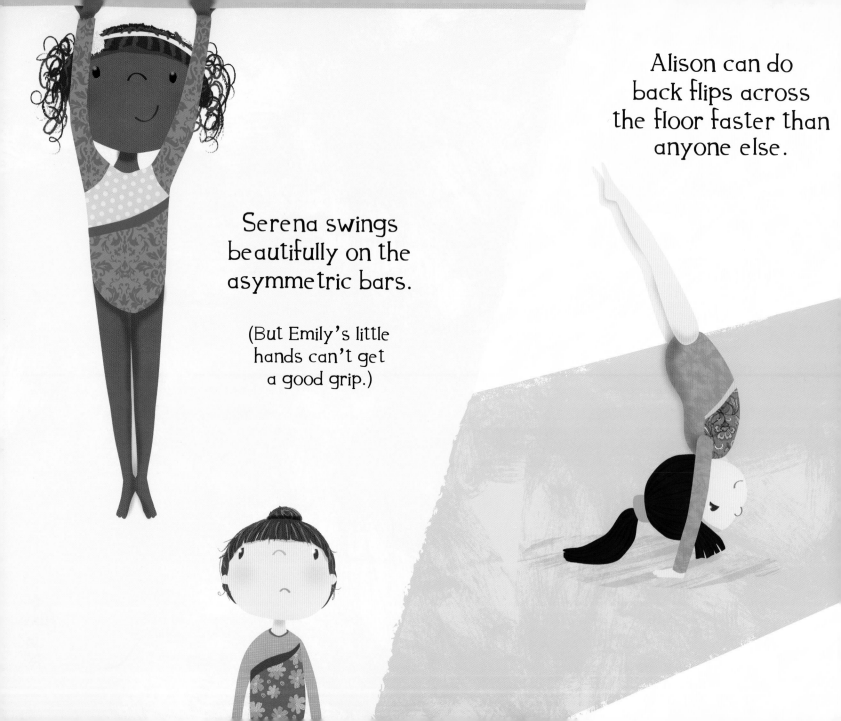

Serena swings
beautifully on the
asymmetric bars.

(But Emily's little
hands can't get
a good grip.)

Alison can do
back flips across
the floor faster than
anyone else.

Sarah vaults
really, really high.

(But Emily can only
do a tiny bounce
from the springboard.)

(But Emily is always
the last to finish.)

Emily still loves gym club,
and she is happy for her friends.
But she wishes that she could
be best at something too.

"I can't even balance on the beam," she thinks sadly,

as she teeters and totters.

"There's **nothing** special about me."

One day, their trainer, Melanie, has some exciting news.

"Our club is taking part in a big gymnastics display," she says.

"We **must** put on a spectacular show!"

Everyone has something
special to do.
Everyone except Emily.

Alison has a special floor
exercise routine with lots
of **handsprings** and leaps.

Serena has a complicated
routine on the asymmetric
bars, with difficult
moves and **twists.**

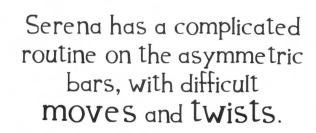

Sarah is picked to perform on the vault.

She makes it
look easy.

"There's something missing," says Melanie.
She closes her eyes and thinks hard.
"We need to finish with a big show-stopper.
I know..."

"We're going to make the **biggest** human pyramid ever!"

All of Emily's friends are in the pyramid.
It gets higher and higher.
"I just need one more gymnast to somersault
down from the very top," says Melanie.
"It needs to be someone light…

someone nimble…

It has to be the smallest
gymnast in the club."

"She . . .
means . . .
ME!"

After weeks of practice,
the day of the display
finally arrives.

Emily and her friends wait
excitedly for the events
to begin.

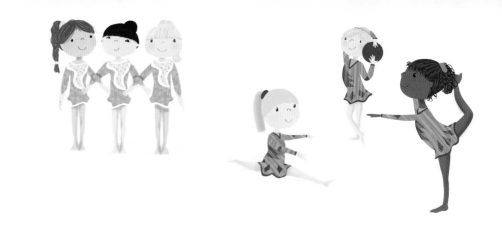

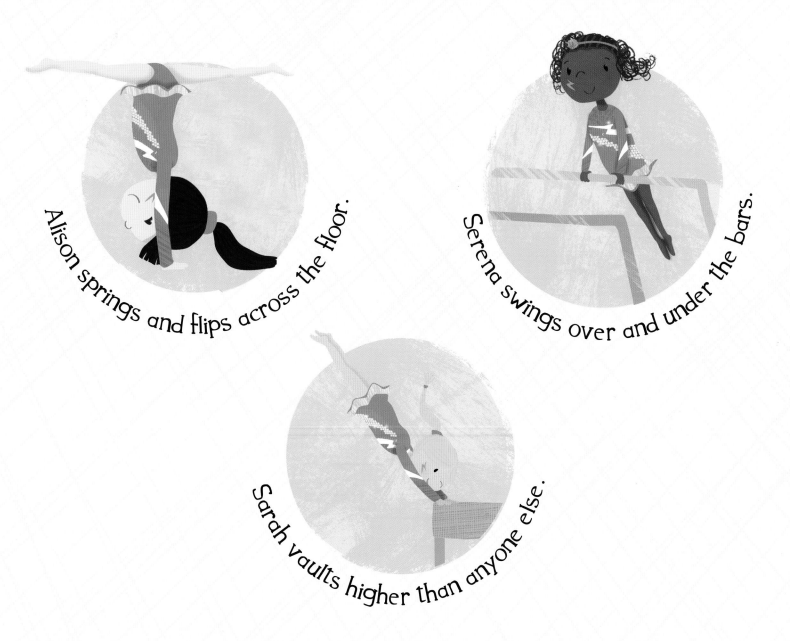

Alison springs and flips across the floor.

Serena swings over and under the bars.

Sarah vaults higher than anyone else.

Then it is time for the show-stopper...

The pyramid is very, very high.

Emily's legs start to wobble when she looks at it.

"I can do this. I can do this!" she says bravely,
and climbs into position at the very top.

Then Emily leaps into
the air and does...

a...

Perfect . . .

somersault!

She lands in the arms of the big gymnast waiting below.

"What a wonderful little gymnast," whispers the judge. Emily is given a special gymnastics necklace for her part in the display.

Emily is still the littlest gymnast of all.
But whenever she looks at her necklace,
she remembers that being little makes her
very, very special!

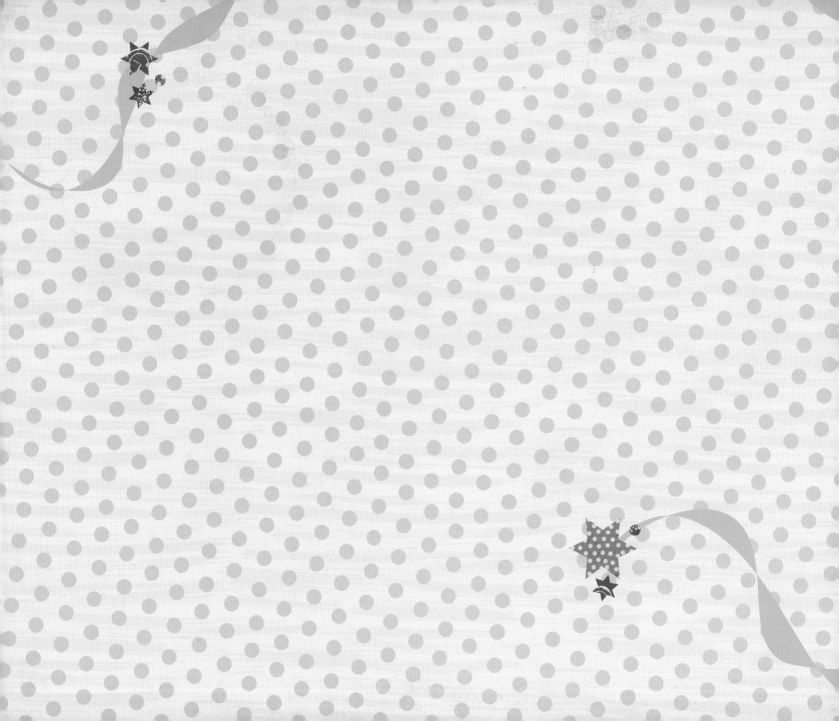